Take Me Out to the Ice Rink

Stella Partheniou Grasso   illustrated by Chris Jones

Scholastic Canada Ltd.

Toronto New York London Auckland Sydney
Mexico City New Delhi Hong Kong Buenos Aires

Scholastic Canada Ltd.
604 King Street West, Toronto, Ontario M5V 1E1, Canada

Scholastic Inc.
557 Broadway, New York, NY 10012, USA

Scholastic Australia Pty Limited
PO Box 579, Gosford, NSW 2250, Australia

Scholastic New Zealand Limited
Private Bag 94407, Botany, Manukau 2163, New Zealand

Scholastic Children's Books
Euston House, 24 Eversholt Street, London NW1 1DB, UK

www.scholastic.ca

Library and Archives Canada Cataloguing in Publication
Partheniou Grasso, Stella, author
Take me out to the ice rink / Stella Partheniou
Grasso; illustrated by Chris Jones.
Story in rhyme.
ISBN 978-1-4431-5725-4 (softcover)
I. Jones, Christopher, illustrator II. Title.
PS8631.A787T35 2017   jC811'.6   C2017-901454-4

6 5 4 3 2   Printed in Malaysia 108   17 18 19 20 21

For Team Grasso: Ross, Nico and Sophia.
Thanks for the assist.
—SPG

To Dad. For showing me the importance of
hard work and a good laugh.
—CJ

Every year when the north winds blow,
We build the boards and pack the snow.
We flood the rink and grab our skates.
We can't wait!
Winter's great!

Hockey season is finally here,
Our favourite season of all the year.
When fans come out and players cheer
In voices loud and clear:

"Take me out to the ice rink.
Take me out to the game.
Pass me my skates and my hockey stick.
I won't quit 'til I score a hat trick.

Let me play, play, play for the home team,
'Cause hockey games are so fun.
For it's one, two, three periods
'til the game's all done."

The puck is dropped; the game is on.

Both teams are pumped and come out strong.

They chase the puck without delay.

Breakaway!

What a play!

In no time flat the visitors score.

Their mascot applauds and calls for more.

We unite like never before

As we take heart and roar:

"Take me out to the ice rink.
Take me out to the game.
They scored first but it's only one goal.
They have the point but we've got the soul.

Let's all cheer, cheer, cheer for the home team.
They're still the best team around.
For we still have two periods,
And we won't back down."

The puck is flying; the play's intense.

Our forward line tears through their defence.

We pass the puck; we're in control.

Spot a hole.

Score a goal!

14

Our players are sharp and hold their ground.
Our next shot misses, but we rebound!
We all rise at the buzzer's sound.
Our cheers spread through the town:

BZZZZZ

"Take me out to the ice rink.
Take me out to the game.
Our superstar players never quit.
That tricky goal showed daring and grit.

Let's all cheer, cheer, cheer for the home team.
We know the game isn't won.
For there's still one more period
'Til the game's all done."

Our players are charged; we're in the lead.
The visiting team starts to stampede.
They charge past and put one in net.
We all sweat.
They're a threat.

The clock is ticking; the stakes are high.
Just one more goal and we'll break the tie.
We steal the puck, aim for the slot,
And make the winning shot.

"Take me out to the ice rink.
Take me out to the game.
We were glued to the edge of our seats
By the players' spectacular feats.

Let's all cheer, cheer, cheer for the home team,
'cause hockey games are so fun.
For it's one, two, three periods,
And the home team won!"